KING ST.

Set Four
THE FIRE

Sid's Story

Sid's Story
King Street: Readers Set Four: The Fire
Copyright © Iris Nunn 2014

Text: Iris Nunn
Editor: June Lewis

Published in 2014 by Gatehouse Media Limited

ISBN: 978-1-84231-136-3

British Library Cataloguing-in-Publication Data:
A catalogue record for this book is available from the British Library

It was hot.
It was dry.
It was one o'clock in the morning.
It was Saturday morning.
It was the morning of August
the tenth.

I was in the bar helping Brenda.
Brenda was washing up.
I was sweeping the floor.

On Friday night we had been full
in the pub.

It was Jill's birthday -
that's Jill from number six.
Jill and Dave had been here
with friends.

They had made a lot of mess -
spilt drinks, crisps everywhere
and cigarette ash on the carpet -
which had to be cleared up.

We were nearly finished
and ready to go to bed.

Brenda went to close the big window.
She called me over.

"What's that smell, Sid?" she said.

I went to the window.
I could smell smoke.
I looked out.

"I think it's the shop," I said.
"I'm going to see."

I looked down the street.
Smoke was coming out of the shop.

I ran back in and rang 999.
"Which service do you want?"
said the man.
I shouted, "Fire!"
I told them to go to King Street -
the corner shop.

"I'm going to look," I said.
"See to Mrs T," said Brenda.

I went down the street
and saw even more smoke.
I banged on the door
and tried to open it.
It was locked.
I saw Mrs T at the window
and so I shouted to her
that there was a lot of smoke
coming from another window upstairs.

Mrs T must have moved fast.
In a short time she was downstairs
and had unlocked the door.
I remember shouting to her,
"There's smoke coming
from one of your rooms!"

"I know, it's Frank's room.
He's still in there and the door's locked,"
she cried back.

I ran up the stairs.
I leaned on the door and pushed.
It would not open.
It was locked.
I ran at the door and pushed again.
I heard the wood splinter.
The door opened
and I fell into the room.

The room was full of smoke.
I could feel the heat.
The smoke stung my eyes.

Through the smoke
I saw Frank on the bed.
I dragged him from the bed
and out onto the landing.
I hoped he was just unconscious
and not dead.

Later on, thank goodness,
he stirred a bit,
after I had dragged him outside.
I have never been so pleased
to see an ambulance.

Mrs T's cup of tea
was one of the best I've ever had.